W9-CZS-496

A Day's Work

by Eve Bunting
Illustrated by Ronald Himler

CLARION BOOKS / New York

Clarion Books
a Houghton Mifflin Company imprint
215 Park Avenue South, New York, NY 10003
Text copyright © 1994 by Eve Bunting
Illustrations copyright © 1994 by Ronald Himler

The illustrations for this book were executed in watercolor and gouache
on Arches 140 lb. hot-press paper.
Type was set in 15/21 pt. Sabon Book.

All rights reserved.

For information about permission to reproduce selections from this book,
write to Permissions, Houghton Mifflin Company,
215 Park Avenue South, New York, NY 10003.

For information about this and other Houghton Mifflin trade and reference
books and multimedia products, visit The Bookstore at Houghton Mifflin
on the World Wide Web at (http://www.hmco.com/trade/).

Printed in the USA

Library of Congress Cataloging-in-Publication Data

Bunting, Eve, 1928–
  A day's work / by Eve Bunting ; illustrated by Ronald Himler.
        p.   cm.
  Summary: When Francisco, a young Mexican American boy, tries to help his
grandfather find work, he discovers that even though the old man cannot speak English,
he has something even more valuable to teach Francisco.
        ISBN 0-395-67321-6   PA ISBN 0-395-84518-1
        [1. Mexican Americans—Fiction.   2. Grandfathers—Fiction.
3. Work —Fiction.   4. Honesty—Fiction.]   I. Himler, Ronald, ill.   II. Title.
PZ7.B91527Dazn 1995
[E]—dc20   93-38357
                                                                                          CIP
                                                                                          AC

HOR   10   9   8   7   6

For Sloan—my Benjamin
—E. B.

For Amy and Dan
—R. H.

Francisco stood in the parking lot with his grandfather and the other men. It was the first time he'd been there.

A truck cruised along, slowed.

The driver held up three fingers. "Bricklaying. I need three men," he called.

Five men jumped in the back.

"Only three," the driver said, and two had to get out.

The workers left in the parking lot grumbled and shuffled around.

Francisco's grandfather shivered. "*Hace frío,*" he said.

"It is cold because it is still early. It will be hot later, you will see," Francisco said in Spanish.

"Why did you bring a kid?" one of the men asked. "No one will hire you with a kid. He belongs in school."

"It's Saturday," Francisco said. "My *abuelo,* my grandfather, does not speak English yet. He came to California only two days ago to live with my mother and me."

Francisco swallowed. "We have been alone—since my father died. I am going to help my *abuelo* get work."

He took his grandfather's cold, rough hand and smiled up at him. Abuelo was tall and skinny as an old tree. Already Francisco loved him. When there was money to spare they'd get him a jacket like Francisco's with sleeves long enough to cover his hands. And an L.A. Lakers cap like Francisco's, too.

A van was coming. BENJAMIN'S GARDENING was printed on the side.

Francisco let go of his grandfather's hand. He darted through the swarm of men and was right in front of the van when it stopped.

"One man," the driver said. "For gardening." He was young, with a thick, black mustache. And he was wearing an L.A. Lakers cap, like Francisco's. Maybe cleaner. It must be an omen, Francisco thought.

"Take us, Mr. Benjamin. *Us.*" Francisco pointed back at his grandfather. He tilted his own cap over his eyes. "Look! We love the Lakers, too. And my grandfather is a fine gardener, though he doesn't know English yet. The gardens are the same, right? Mexican and American?"

Francisco waved urgently for his grandfather to come. "Also, you will get two for one," he said. "I don't charge for my work."

The man grinned. "OK. I'm convinced. But I'm not Mr. Benjamin. Call me Ben."

He motioned to Francisco. "You and your grandfather jump in back. Sixty dollars for the day."

Francisco nodded. His breath was coming fast. That much for a day's work? Mama would be so happy. Her job didn't pay much. There'd be extra food tonight, maybe chorizos.

He pulled open the back door, threw in the bag of lunch Mama had packed, and hurried his grandfather into the van ahead of him.

A big, tough guy tried to get in, too. Francisco pushed him back. *He* was tough. He was a worker.

"It is gardening," he told Abuelo as the van pulled away.

"But I do not know gardening. I am a carpenter. I have always lived in the city."

"It is easy." Francisco waved through the window at the passing cars. "Flowers, roses, things like that." He raised his cap to a lady in a car. "*Señora,*" he said politely, though she couldn't hear.

The van turned off the freeway onto a winding road and stopped. A sloping bank led up to the backyards of new houses. Some were not yet finished. Workers climbed high on rooftops and there was the good smell of tar.

The high bank was dotted with pretty white flowers and overgrown with coarse green spikes. Six big black trash cans waited below.

They all got out of the van but Ben left the motor running.

"I need you to weed this bank," he told Abuelo. "Be sure to get the roots." He pointed to the cans. "Dump them here."

"Good. Fine." It was Francisco who answered.

"I have another job to go to," Ben said. "I'll pick you up at three. It will be hot. Your grandfather will need a hat." He took a straw one from the van.

"*Grácias*," Abuelo said.

"See you guys then. Work hard. Have a nice day."

"What did he say?" Abuelo asked as the van drove off.

"He said to have a nice day. It is what everyone says up here."

"Your English is very good, my grandson," Abuelo said.

Francisco nodded and smiled. He climbed the bank and hung his jacket on a railing. "Now," he said. "I will show you." He pulled up one of the spiky clumps and shook the dirt from its roots. "These are weeds. Do not touch the flowers."

His grandfather smiled. "*Bueno*." Francisco could see his strong white teeth all the way to the back.

They worked through the morning.

A little poodle barked at them through the railings above. "Yap, yap, yap."

An orange cat prowled the bank.

There was a pool in one of the new backyards. Francisco heard splashing and voices. The water sounds made him hotter. His shoulders and arms hurt. He thought about how proud Mama would be tonight.

"Sixty dollars?" she'd say, and she'd hug Francisco and Abuelo. "It is a fortune."

At lunchtime he and Abuelo ate the tortillas and tomatoes and drank the bottle of water she had packed.

In another hour they were finished.

The bank looked so nice with just the brown dirt and the pretty flowers.

"*Muy bonito*," Abuelo said.

And Francisco said, "Yes, beautiful!"

He and his grandfather shook hands.

Francisco thought he had never felt so good. He'd helped his grandfather and he had worked himself.

They sat on the curb to wait for the van, and when it came they stood and brushed the loose dirt from their clothes.

21

Ben got out and stared up at the bank. "Holy Toledo!" he said.

"You didn't think we could do such a good job?" Francisco wanted to laugh, Ben seemed so shocked.

Francisco gave a little jump and pretended to slam dunk a ball. "Like the Lakers. We work hard."

"I can't believe it!" Ben whispered. "You . . . you took out all the plants and left the weeds."

Francisco stepped closer to Abuelo. "But the flowers . . ." he began.

Ben pointed. "Those flowers are chickweed. Chickweed! You took out my young ice plants." He yanked off his Lakers cap and slammed it against the van.

"What is it? Did we do something wrong?" Abuelo whispered in Spanish to Francisco.

Ben's mustache quivered with anger. "I thought you said your grandfather was a fine gardener. He doesn't even know a *chickweed?*"

Abuelo looked from one of them to the other. "Tell me what is happening, Francisco," he said.

"We left the weeds. We took out the plants," Francisco said softly in Spanish. It was hard to look at his grandfather as he spoke.

"He thought we knew about gardening," Abuelo said. His Spanish was fast and angry. "You lied to him. Isn't that so?"

"We needed a day's work. . . ."

"We do not lie for work."

Now there was more sadness than anger in Abuelo's voice. "Ah, my grandson." He put a hand on Francisco's shoulder. "Ask him what we can do. Tell him we will come back tomorrow, if he agrees. We will pull out the weeds and put the good plants back."

Francisco felt his heart go weak. "But . . . but Abuelo, that will be twice the work. And tomorrow is Sunday. There is a Lakers game on TV. And there is also church." He hoped the word *church* would perhaps change his grandfather's thinking.

"We will miss them both, then," his grandfather said. "It is the price of the lie. Tell the gentleman what I said and ask him if the plants will live."

Ben said they would. "The roots are still there. If they're replanted early, they'll be all right."

He rubbed his eyes. "This is partly my fault. I should have stayed to get you started. But tell your grandfather I appreciate his offer and I'll bring you back in the morning."

The three of them got in the van.

Francisco sat by the window in huddled silence. He didn't wave to passing cars. He didn't raise his cap. He'd helped his grandfather find work. But in the end the lie had spoiled the day. His throat burned with tears.

The parking lot was empty. The trash can overflowed with used paper cups and sandwich wrappings.

Ben let them out.

"Look," he said. "If you need money I'll give you half now." He began to pull his wallet from his pocket but Abuelo held up his hand.

"Tell him we take the pay tomorrow, when we finish."

Francisco's grandfather and Ben looked at each other and words seemed to pass between them, though there were no words. Ben slid his wallet back into his pocket.

Francisco sighed. The lie had taken the chorizos, too.

"Tomorrow then. Six A.M.," Ben said. "And tell your grandfather I can always use a good man—for more than just one day's work."

Francisco gave a hop of excitement. More than just a day's work!

Ben was still speaking. "The important things your grandfather knows already. And I can teach him gardening."

Francisco nodded. He understood. He would tell his grandfather, and he would tell him something else. He, Francisco, had begun to learn the important things, too.

Francisco took his grandfather's cold, rough hand in his. "Let's go home, Abuelo," he said.